# THE ABBA TREE

By Devora Busheri

Illustrations by Gal Shkedi

KAR-BEN
PUBLISHING

For my four sweethearts, and for their Abba —D.B.

For my beloved family —G.S.

KAR-BEN PUBLISHING®
An imprint of Lerner Publishing Group, Inc.
241 First Avenue North
Minneapolis, MN 55401 USA

Website address: www.karben.com

Main body text set in Excelsior LT Std
Typeface provided by Adobe Systems

**Library of Congress Cataloging-in-Publication Data**

Names: Busheri, Devora, 1967– author. | Shkedi, Gal, illustrator.
Title: The Abba tree / Devora Busheri ; illustrated by Gal Shkedi.
Description: Minneapolis : Kar-Ben Publishing, [2020] | Series:
   Tu B'Shevat | Audience: Ages 4–9. | Audience: Grades K–1. |
   Summary: While her father naps nearby, Hannah searches for
   the perfect tree to climb.
Identifiers: LCCN 2019041616 (print) | LCCN 2019041617 (ebook) |
   ISBN 9781541534667 (library binding) | ISBN 9781541534759
   (paperback) | ISBN 9781541599628 (ebook)
Subjects: CYAC: Trees—Fiction. | Tree climbing—Fiction. |
   Tu bi-Shevat—Fiction. | Fathers and daughters—Fiction.
Classification: LCC PZ7.1.B8877 Ab 2020  (print) | LCC PZ7.1.B8877
   (ebook) | DDC [E]—dc23

LC record available at https://lccn.loc.gov/2019041616
LC ebook record available at https://lccn.loc.gov/2019041617

PJ Library Edition ISBN 978-1-72842-394-4

Manufactured in China
1-49196-49323-3/23/2020

102032.6K/B1544/A4

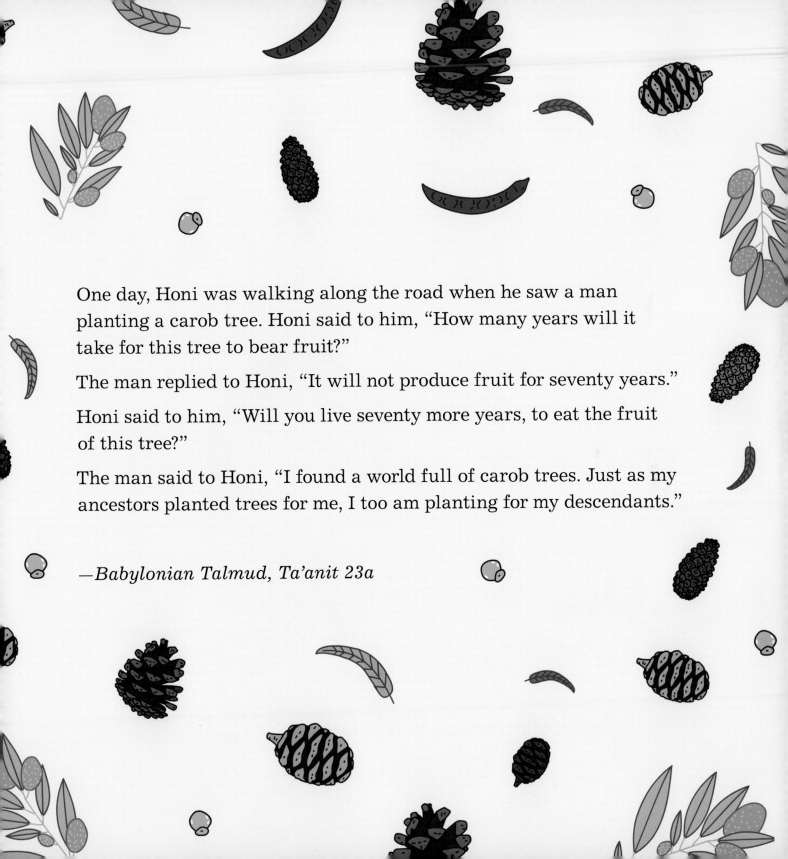

One day, Honi was walking along the road when he saw a man planting a carob tree. Honi said to him, "How many years will it take for this tree to bear fruit?"

The man replied to Honi, "It will not produce fruit for seventy years."

Honi said to him, "Will you live seventy more years, to eat the fruit of this tree?"

The man said to Honi, "I found a world full of carob trees. Just as my ancestors planted trees for me, I too am planting for my descendants."

—*Babylonian Talmud, Ta'anit 23a*

"Abba, I want a tree to climb," said Hannah.

"So plant one," said Abba. "Tu B'Shevat is coming soon."

Hannah laughed. "But I want to climb a tree *now*," she said.

"And I want to *sleep* now." Abba leaned on the thin trunk of the carob tree. It was a young tree, and it spread very little shade over Abba, but Hannah knew that the carob tree was his favorite.

"Oh, Abba, don't fall asleep now," said Hannah.

She looked around, seeking a tree to climb.

The eucalyptus tree was the tallest of them all. Beneath it, bell-shaped seed pods were scattered on the soft bark peels that covered the ground.

"*This* will be my tree," thought Hannah, and ran off to climb it right away. Because when you want something, now is better than not-now.

Hannah held on tight to the gray-green tree trunk. The trunk was slippery, and her hands slid off. She looked around in search of another tree to climb.

Beyond the eucalyptus tree stood a pine tree. Its pinecones were scattered around like little balls waiting to play.

"*This* will be my tree," thought Hannah. She stepped over to its trunk, the pine needles crackling delightfully beneath her feet. She held on tight to the wide trunk, but its bark was rough and scratchy against her hands.

Hannah looked around again.

The olive tree was patiently waiting.
Its trunk was full of dents and knobs
and tiny hollows. How wonderful! Hannah
immediately placed her foot on one of the knobs,
held on tight to a branch, and heaved herself all the
way to the top of the tree!

"Abba!" Hannah knew Abba was not really sleeping.

"Mmm . . ." said Abba, with one eye closed.

"I did it! Abba! I—ahh—AHH—*ACHOO*!"

Tiny pollen from the tree tickled Hannah's nose and she came tumbling down.

Hannah looked around, but there were no more trees to climb.
Only the young carob, whose branches were thin and fragile.

Hannah stood next to Abba. "Abba! I want a tree to climb!"

Abba opened his eyes. "I told you," he smiled. "Plant one."
Abba winked at Hannah. A joyful
wink, a golden wink, a wink that
tickled all the rays of the sun.

"Plant an Abba Tree."

"Just in time for Tu B'Shevat!" laughed Hannah,
   and she gleefully began . . .

She firmly planted two feet. Roots.

She spread out Abba's two arms. Abba's arms were strong.

Then she bent two knee-knobs.

Finally she tousled the treetop hair and made sure the neck was very, very tall.

"An Abba Tree." Hannah was pleased. "Not too slippery, and not too scratchy.

"Just perfect

for me

to climb . . ."

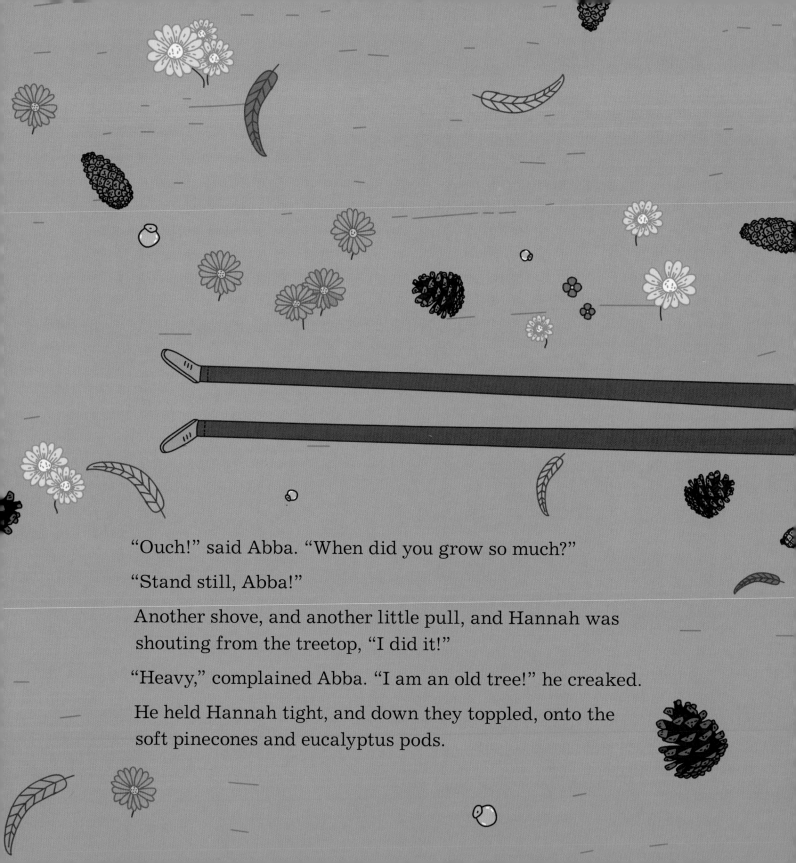

"Ouch!" said Abba. "When did you grow so much?"

"Stand still, Abba!"

Another shove, and another little pull, and Hannah was
shouting from the treetop, "I did it!"

"Heavy," complained Abba. "I am an old tree!" he creaked.

He held Hannah tight, and down they toppled, onto the
soft pinecones and eucalyptus pods.

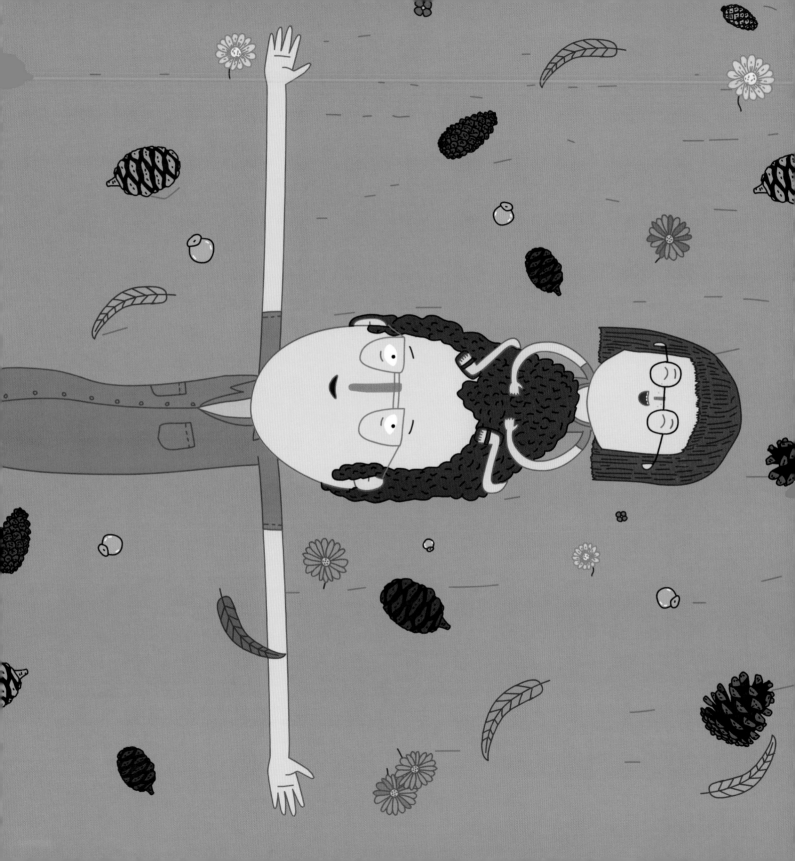

Hannah and Abba rested against the carob tree.

"When did you plant this carob tree, Abba?" Hannah asked.

"Many Tu B'Shevats ago," said Abba. "In the year you were born."

Hannah knew the answer, but she loved to hear it.

"When can we eat the carob's fruit?" Hannah asked. She felt her eyes closing in the golden sun.

"Not this Tu B'Shevat," said Abba. "Only in many, many years to come."

"So why did we plant it?"
Hannah asked, nodding off to sleep.

"Because when you came into this world it was full
of trees," whispered Abba. "And we wanted to leave
a world full of trees for your children."

He knew Hannah couldn't hear him.

On the ground, in the warm air, beneath the shade of the
eucalyptus tree, the pine tree, the olive tree and the carob
tree, Hannah was fast asleep.

## ABOUT THE AUTHOR AND ILLUSTRATOR

**Devora Busheri** is a children's book writer, editor, and translator. She has authored and edited many books for various publication houses in Israel. Her books include *My Sister is Sleeping* and *In the Jerusalem Forest*. Devora lives in Jerusalem with her husband and their four children.

**Gal Shkedi** is an animation director, illustrator, and character designer based in Tel Aviv, Israel.